W9-AAZ-768

3 1526 05138615 6

Mamaqtuq!

Titiraqtuq Paiggaalaqautikkut · Titiqtugaqtuq Iurik Kim

Written by The Jerry Cans · Illustrated by Eric Kim

Published by Inhabit Media Inc.
www.inhabitmedia.com

Inhabit Media Inc. (Iqaluit) P.O. Box 11125, Iqaluit, Nunavut, X0A 1H0
(Toronto) 191 Eglinton Ave. East, Suite 310, Toronto, Ontario, M4P 1K1

Design and layout copyright © 2018, 2017 by Inhabit Media Inc.
Text copyright © 2018, 2017 by The Jerry Cans
Illustrations by Eric Kim copyright © 2018, 2017 Inhabit Media Inc.

Based on characters designed by Steve Rigby

Edited by Neil Christopher and Louise Flaherty
Art direction by Danny Christopher
Design by Astrid Arijanto
Digital colours by Astrid Arijanto

All rights reserved. The use of any part of this publication reproduced, transmitted in any form or by any means, electronic, mechanical, photocopying, recording, or otherwise, or stored in a retrievable system, without written consent of the publisher, is an infringement of copyright law.

This project was made possible in part by the Government of Canada.

We acknowledge the support of the Canada Council for the Arts for our publishing program.

Printed and bound in Canada

Library and Archives Canada Cataloguing in Publication

Jerry Cans (Musical group), author
Mamaqtuq! / titiraqtuq Paiggaalaqautikkut ; titiqtugaqtuq Iurik Kim = Mamaqtuq! / written by The Jerry Cans ; illustrated by Eric Kim.

Text in romanized Inuktitut and English.
ISBN 978-1-77227-230-7 (hardcover)

1. Songs, Inuktitut–Canada–Texts. 2. Songs, English–Canada–Texts. I. Kim, Eric, 1977-, illustrator II. Jerry Cans (Musical group). Mamaqtuq! III. Jerry Cans (Musical group). Mamaqtuq! English. IV. Title.

PS8619.E77M36 2018 jC813'.6 C2018-904637-6

Mamaqtuq!

Titiraqtuq Paiggaalaqautikkut · Titiqtugaqtuq Iurik Kim

Written by The Jerry Cans · Illustrated by Eric Kim

Ullaakkut Naggajjaumi, umiaqtulauqtugut.

Early on Monday morning, we went out boating.

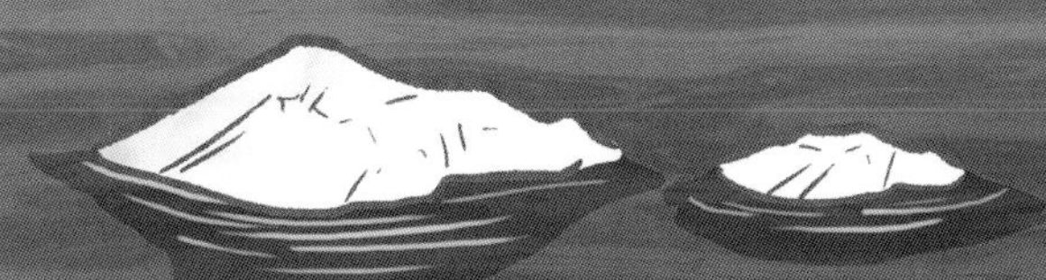

Sila Qanuilauqpa? Silattiavaulauqtuq!

How was the weather? It was a beautiful day!

Imaq qanuilauqpa? Uqsualauqtuq!

And how was the water? Smooth, and shimmering in the sunshine!

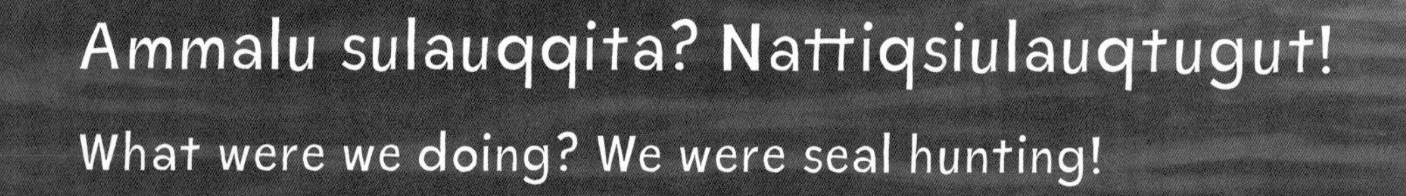

Ammalu sulauqqita? Nattiqsiulauqtugut!

What were we doing? We were seal hunting!

Mamaqtuq, mamaqtuq! Nattiminiq uujuq!

Delicious, so delicious! Seal stew!

Unnusakkut Naggajjaumi, suli nattiqsiulauqtugut.

In the afternoon, we were still out seal hunting.

Akunialuk qikalauqtugut, upirngassaangutillugu quvianaqtuq!

We waited and waited. Springtime is the most beautiful time of the year!

Kisiani suli nattiqqaunngittugut!

But we still couldn't catch a seal!

Unnusakkut suli nattiqsiulauqtugut.

In the afternoon, we were still seal hunting.

Kaalauqtugut. Palaugaaqanngittugut. Tiiqanngittugut.

We started to get hungry. We ran out of bannock. We ran out of tea.

Usuujaralaaqanngittugut. Nikkuqanngittugut!

We ran out of hot dogs. We ran out of jerky!

Unnukkut Naggajjaumi, suli nattiqsiulauqtugut.

Late into the evening, we continued to hunt.

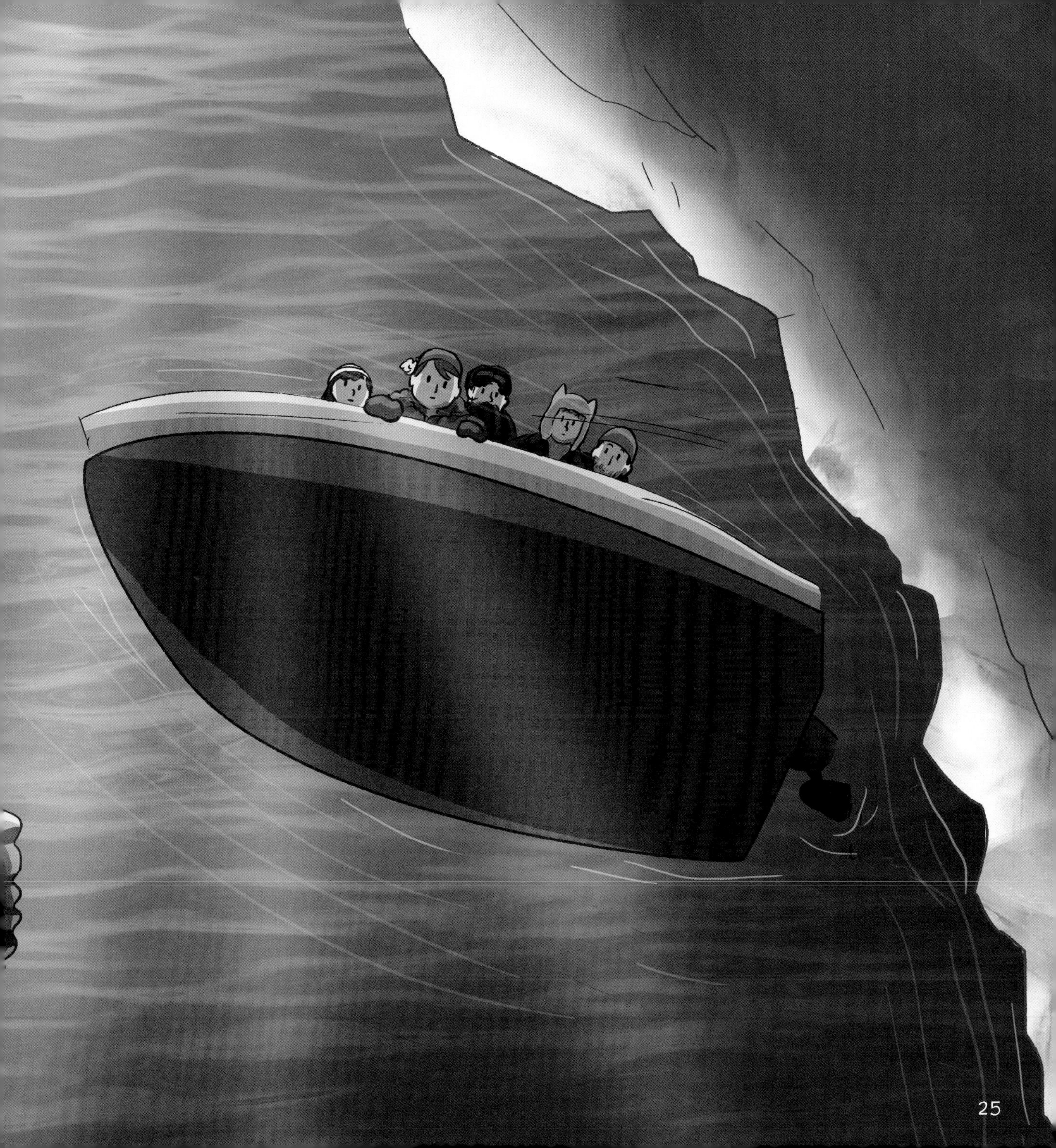

Qanurluu? Qanuq? Nattiqsilauqtugut!

Then you know what? What? We saw a young seal!

Nattiakuluk puilauqtuq qukilauqtara.

The young seal surfaced and I shot it . . . .

Pilattugu nirilauqtugut alianait!

Then we cut it up and enjoyed a delicious meal. What an amazing day!

Nijjausijaqtiit

Sukattumik quviagijallariit ukiuqtaqtumi Paiggaalaqautikkut inngigaliusuut kajungiqsuqtaullutik nunaminni Iqalunni, Nunavuumi. Ajjiunngitturmik katiqsuisimallutik Inuktitut qimuksiutiliktitut, kattajjarnirmik, ammalu qirniqtait nijjausijautingit. Paiggaalaqautikkut ukiuqtaqturmiutallariit ajjigijaunngitsiaqsutik. Taakkua inngiqtiit inngiqattasuut amisunik Inuktitut, aksuruutiqatsiaqsutillu papatsigiaqarnirmik Inuktitut uqausirmik ukiuqtaqtuq nunalingallu asijjiqpalliagaluaqtillugu. Ukiuqtaqturmiunik kiggaqtuigumallariktut tukisititsitsiarumallutillu imainniraqtauninginnik qaujisimajarminnik ukiuqtaqturmiut inuusingita; inngigangit isumatsaqsiurnaqtut/ tukisititsilutillu maannauliqtuq ukiuqtaqturmi, inunginnillu tunngaviqaqtunik tarnirminnik. Pijjutituaqanngittut gavamatigut aulajurnik, kisianili sukattummarimmik qaujimajauliramik inummariillu uvikkaillu mumiqattaqtut ippigijauliqtut inunnut uummarittummariummata. Taakkua nijjausijaqtiit malittitsiniaqtut ilinnik Iqaluit aturiangitigut pisuqatiqarlutik takuqqujjitillugit inuusiujuq ukiuqtaqtumi qanuimmangaat.

Aannuluu Muarisan (inngiqti/kukkittapaaqti)
Naansi Maik (inngititsijuq/katajjaqtuq)
Jiina Vuurjas (agiagaqtuq)
Vurintan Tuati (kukkittapaaqtuq qatitujurmut)
Stiiv Rigvi (anautsagaqtuq)

The Band

The fast-rising Northern stars The Jerry Cans create music inspired by their hometown of Iqaluit, Nunavut. With their unique mix of Inuktitut alt-country, throat singing, and reggae, The Jerry Cans are a distinctly Northern, one-of-a-kind group. The band members perform many of their songs in Inuktitut and are passionate about preserving the language even as the North and their home community of Iqaluit evolve. They are committed to representing Northerners and to challenging common misperceptions they have encountered about life in the Arctic; their music evokes the contemporary North and the spirited people who reside there. It is not only their political motives, but their rapidly developing reputation for getting elders and young people dancing, that has forced people to start noticing this high-energy group. This truly unique band will take you on a stroll through the streets of Iqaluit to share a glimpse of life in the Arctic.

Andrew Morrison (Vocals/Guitar)
Nancy Mike (Accordion/Throat Singing)
Gina Burgess (Violin)
Brendan Doherty (Bass)
Steve Rigby (Drums)

Iurik Kim titiqtugaqti, kaamiknik takuminaqtuliuqti titiqtugarnillu aulajuunik. Titiqtugaqpaktangita ilangit *Aul Maagasiin*, Singking Sip Iantutainmint Saapturhaus Kaamiks, titiqtugarataaqtaviningit *Nuatgaart*. Nuliariik Turaantumiutaak Kanatamit.

Eric Kim is an illustrator, comic artist, and animator. His illustration work includes *Owl Magazine*, Sinking Ship Entertainment, and Chapterhouse Comics, where he most recently illustrated *Northguard*. He lives with his wife in Toronto, Canada.

www.inhabitmedia.com